D

D1437151

Daphne
du Maurier

HAPPY CHRISTMAS

Daphne
du Maurier

HAPPY CHRISTMAS

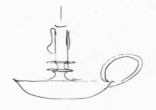

C

CENTURY

HAPPY CHRISTMAS
is published by
Century Publishing Co. Ltd
Portland House
12-13 Greek Street
London W1V 5LE

ISBN: 0-7126-0962-8

First published in November 1942
by Todd Publishing Co., London

© Daphne du Maurier 1942, 1984

Devised and produced by
Michael Balfour Ltd
3 Wedgwood Mews
Greek Street
London W1V 5LW

Jacket illustration Sarah John
Decorations Dana Balfour
Designers Anthony Lawrence & Hilly Beavan
Printed by St Edmundsbury Press,
Bury St Edmunds, Suffolk
Bound by Hunter & Foulis Ltd, Edinburgh

T he Lawrence family lived in a large house just outside town. Mr Lawrence was a big, heavy man, with a round face and a smile. He motored into town every day to his office, where he had a roll-top desk and three secretaries. During the day he used the telephone, and had a business lunch, and then used the telephone again. He made a lot of money.

Mrs Lawrence had fair hair and china-blue eyes. Mr Lawrence called her Kitten, but she was not helpless. She had a lovely figure and long fingernails, and she played bridge most afternoons. Bob Lawrence was ten. He was like Mr Lawrence, only smaller. He was fond of electric trains, and his father had got some men to fix up a miniature railway in the garden. Marigold Lawrence was seven. She was like her mother, only rounder. She had fifteen dolls. She kept breaking them somehow.

If you met them anywhere you would not recognize the Lawrences as being different from any other family. Perhaps that was the trouble. They were just a bit too much like all the rest. Life was a comfortable and an easy thing, which was, of course, very pleasant.

On Christmas Eve the Lawrence family did much the same as every other family. Mr Lawrence came home early from town so that he could stand around and watch the household get ready for tomorrow. He smiled more than usual and put his hands in his pockets and shouted, "Look out, you damn fool!" when he tripped over the dog who was hiding behind some evergreen. Mrs Lawrence had cut bridge for once and was threading lanterns across the drawing room. Actually it was the garden boy who threaded the lanterns, but Mrs Lawrence stuck little frills of coloured paper round them and handed them to him, and as she was smoking all the time the smoke got in the garden boy's eyes, but he was too polite to brush it away. Bob Lawrence and Marigold Lawrence kept running round the drawing room and jumping onto the sofas and chairs and calling out "What am I going to have tomorrow? Am I going to have a train? Am I going to have a doll?" until Mr Lawrence got fed up and said, "If you don't stop that row you won't get anything," but he said it in a way that did not mean much, and the children were not deceived.

It was just before the children's bedtime that Mrs Lawrence was called to the telephone. She said "Damn!", and some more smoke got into the garden boy's eyes. Mr Lawrence picked up a piece of evergreen and stuck it behind a picture. He whistled cheerfully.

Mrs Lawrence was away five minutes, and when she came back her blue eyes were full of sparks and her hair was rumpled. She looked like a kitten. The kind you pick up and say "Sweet Puss!" to and then quickly put down again.

"Oh, it's a bit thick, it really is," she said, and for a moment the children thought she was going to cry.

"What the hell's the matter?" asked Mr Lawrence.

"It's that refugee officer for the district," said Mrs Lawrence. "You know — I told you the place was swarming with refugees. Well, like everybody else, I had to put our names down as receivers when the thing started, never thinking seriously

8

that anything would happen. And now it has. We've got to take in a couple, here tonight."

Mr Lawrence stopped smiling. "Look here," he said, "the refugee officer can't do that sort of thing to people without proper warning. Why didn't you tell him to go to blazes?"

"I did," said Mrs Lawrence indignantly, "and all he could say was that he was very sorry, but it was the same for everybody, and people in every house were having to do it, and he said something about a 'compulsory measure' which I did not understand, but it sounded nasty."

"They can't do it," said Mr Lawrence, sticking out his jaw. "I'll get on the phone to someone in authority, I'll see that officer is sacked, I'll go into town myself, I'll —"

"Oh, what's the use?" said Mrs Lawrence. "Don't let's get ourselves all heated over it. You forget it's Christmas Eve and everyone's out of town by now. Anyway, the creatures are on their way, and we can't very well lock the doors. I suppose I shall have to break it to the servants."

"What will the refugees do?" clamoured the children excitedly. "Will they want to take our things? Will they want our beds?"

"Of course not," said Mrs Lawrence sharply. "Don't be such little idiots!"

"Where are we going to put them?" asked Mr Lawrence. "We shall have every room full as it is, with the Dalys and the Collinses coming over tomorrow. You surely don't suggest we put them off now?"

"No fear," said Mrs Lawrence, her

blue eyes sparkling. "That's one comfort, we can truthfully say the house *is* full. No, the refugees can have the room over the garage. It's been very dry up to now, so the damp won't have got through. There is a bed there that we turned out of the house two months ago — the springs had gone. But there's nothing wrong with it. And I think the servants have an oil stove they don't use."

Mr Lawrence smiled. "You've got it all taped, haven't you?" he said. "No one can get the better of you, Kitten. Oh well, as long as it doesn't hurt us, I don't care." He swooped down in sudden relief and picked up Marigold. "Anyway, we won't let it spoil our Christmas, will we, honey?" he said. And he tossed Marigold in the air, and she shrieked with laughter.

"It's not fair," said Bob Lawrence, his round face flushed. "Marigold is younger than me and she wants to hang up the same size stocking. I'm eldest, I ought to have the biggest, oughtn't I?"

Mr Lawrence rumpled his son's hair. "Be a man, Bob," he said, "and don't tease your sister. I've got something for you tomorrow better than any toy you'll find in your stocking."

Bob stopped scowling. "Is it something for my railway?" he asked eagerly.

Mr Lawrence winked and would not answer.

Bob began to jump up and down on his bed. "My present's going to be bigger than Marigold's," he shouted in triumph, "much, much bigger."

"It's not, it's not," cried Marigold tearfully. "Mine is just as nice, isn't it

Dad?"

Mr Lawrence called to the nurse: "Come and quieten the kids, will you? I think they're getting too excited." He laughed and went down the stairs.

Mrs Lawrence met him halfway. "They've arrived," she said. Her voice had a warning note.

"Well?" he asked.

She shrugged her shoulders and made a little face. "Jews," she said briefly — and went into the nursery.

Mr Lawrence said something, and then he straightened his tie and put on an expression that he considered right for refugees. It was a mixture of sternness and bravado. He went round the drive to the garage and climbed the rickety stairs.

"Ha, good evening!" he said in loud, jovial tones as he entered the room. "Are you fixed up all right?"

The room was rather dim, for the one electric light bulb had not been dusted for many months and it hung in one corner, away from the bed and the table and the stove. The two refugees stared for a moment without speaking. The woman was sitting at the table, unpacking a basket, from which she brought a loaf of bread and two cups. The man was spreading a blanket over the bed, and, when Mr Lawrence spoke, he straightened his back and turned towards him.

"We are so grateful," he said, "so very grateful."

Mr Lawrence coughed and half-laughed. "Oh, that's all right," he said. "No trouble at all."

They were Jews and no mistake. The man's nose was enormous, and his skin that typical 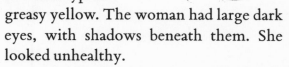 greasy yellow. The woman had large dark eyes, with shadows beneath them. She looked unhealthy.

"Er — anything else you want?" asked Mr Lawrence.

The woman answered this time. She shook her head, "We want nothing," she said. "We are very tired."

"Everywhere was full," said the man. "No one could take us in. It is most generous of you."

"Not at all, not at all," said Mr Lawrence, waving his hand. "Good thing we had this room empty. You must have had a stiff time where you've been."

They said nothing to this.

"Well," said Mr Lawrence, "if there's nothing more I can do, I'll say good night. Don't forget to turn the stove down if it smokes. And — er — if you should need more food or blankets or anything, just give a knock on the back door and ask the servants. Good night."

"Good night," they echoed, and then the woman added, "A Happy Christmas to you."

Mr Lawrence stared. "Oh yes," he said, "Yes, of course. Thanks very much."

He turned up the collar of his coat as he walked round to the front door. It was cold. There would be a sharp frost. The gong was just sounding for dinner as he went into the hall. The garden boy had finished stringing up the lanterns, and they fluttered from the ceiling with a jaunty air. Mrs Lawrence was mixing a drink at the table by the fire.

"Hurry up," she called over her shoulder, "dinner will be spoilt, and if there's anything I loathe it's lukewarm duck."

"Kids asleep?" asked Mr Lawrence.

"I shouldn't think so," said Mrs Lawrence. "It's difficult to get them to settle on Christmas Eve. I gave them both some chocolate and told them to be quiet. Want a drink?"

Later, when they were undressing for the night, Mr Lawrence poked his head round from the dressing room, a toothbrush in his hand.

"Funny thing," he said, "that woman wished me a Happy Christmas. I never knew the Jews kept Christmas before."

"I don't suppose she knows what it means," said Mrs Lawrence, and she patted some skin food into her round, smooth cheek.

One by one the lights in the house were extinguished. The Lawrence family slept. Outside, the sky was bright with stars. And, in the room over the garage, there was one light burning.

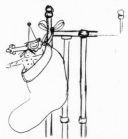

"I say, gosh, just look at this, I've got an aeroplane as well as a new engine for my railway," shouted Bob. "Look, it works like a real one. Look at the propeller."

"Have I got two things from Dad as well?" asked Marigold fumbling feverishly amongst the litter of paper on her bed, and she threw aside the large doll she had just unpacked. "Nurse," she shrieked, "where's my other present from Dad?" Her cheeks were hot and flushed.

"Serves you right for being so greedy," mocked Bob. "Look what I've got."

"I'll break your silly horrid plane," said Marigold, and tears began to fall down her cheeks.

"You mustn't quarrel on Christmas Day," said Nurse, and she drew a small box triumphantly from the heap of waste paper. "Look, Marigold, what's in here?"

Marigold tore aside the paper. Soon she held a glittering necklace in her hands. "I'm a princess!" she shouted. "I'm a princess!"

Bob threw her a glance of contempt. "It's not very big," he said.

Downstairs Mr and Mrs Lawrence were being served with their morning tea. The electric stove was lit, the curtains drawn, and the room was flooded with sunlight. The letters and the parcels remained unopened, though, for both Mr and Mrs Lawrence listened aghast to the tale that Anna, the servant, had to tell.

"I can't believe it, it's preposterous," said Mr Lawrence.

"I can. It's just typical of the sort of thing these people do," said Mrs Lawrence.

"Won't I give that refugee officer hell!" said Mr Lawrence.

"I don't suppose he knew," said Mrs Lawrence. "They took jolly good care not to let on that anything might happen. Well, we can't keep them here now, that's certain. There's no one here to look after the woman."

"We must telephone for an ambulance and have them removed," said Mr Lawrence. "I thought the woman had a bad colour. She must be pretty tough to have stood it, all alone."

"Oh, those sort of people have babies very easily," said Mrs Lawrence. "They scarcely feel it. Well, I'm very thankful they were in the garage room and not in the house. They can't have done much damage there."

"And, Anna," she called, as the maid was leaving the room, "be sure and tell Nurse that the children are not to go near the garage until the ambulance has been."

Then they settled down to the letters and parcels.

"We'll make everyone laugh at the story, anyway," said Mr Lawrence. "It will go down well with the turkey and the plum pudding."

When they had breakfasted and had dressed, and the children had been in to tumble about on the beds and show their presents, Mr and Mrs Lawrence went round to the garage to see what could be done about the refugees. The children were sent up to the nursery to play with their new things, because, after all, what had happened was not very nice, as Nurse agreed with Mrs Lawrence. And besides, you never knew.

When they came to the garage they found a little crowd of servants in the yard talking. There were the cook, and the parlour man, and one of the housemaids, and the chauffeur, and even the garden boy.

"What's going on?" asked Mr Lawrence.

"They've cleared out," said the chauffeur.

"How do you mean, cleared out?"

"The fellow went off while we were having breakfast and got hold of a taxi," said the chauffeur. "He must have gone to the stand at the end of the road. Never a word to any of us."

"And we heard wheels by the back gate," chimed in the cook, "and he and the taxi driver were lifting the woman into the car."

"The fellow asked for the name of a hospital, and we told him there was a Jewish hospital just before you get into town," said the chauffeur. "He said he was very sorry to have given us all this trouble. Cool sort of customer, hadn't turned a hair."

"And the baby. We saw the baby," giggled the housemaid, and then she blushed furiously for no reason.

"Yes," said the cook, "a proper little Jew, the image of his father."

And then they all laughed and looked at one another rather foolishly.

"Well," said Mr Lawrence, "there's

nothing more any of us can do, I suppose."

The servants melted away. The excitement for the moment was over. There was the Christmas party to prepare for, and what with one thing and another they felt they had been run off their legs already, and it was only ten o'clock.

"We'd better have a look," said Mr Lawrence, jerking his head at the garage. Mrs Lawrence made a face and followed him.

They climbed the rickety stairs to the little dark room in the loft. There was no sign of disorder. The bed had been placed back against the wall, and the blanket was neatly folded at the foot. The chair and table were in the usual place. The window in the room had been opened to let in the fresh morning air. The stove had been turned out. Only one thing showed that the room had been used. On the floor, beside the bed, was a glass of cold water.

Mr Lawrence did not say anything. Mrs Lawrence did not say anything, either. They went back to the house and into the drawing room. Mr Lawrence wandered to the window and looked out across the garden. He could see Bob's miniature railway at the far corner. Mrs Lawrence opened a parcel she had not seen at breakfast. Overhead, shouts and yells told that the children were either enjoying themselves or not.

"What about your golf? Weren't you meeting the others at eleven?" asked Mrs Lawrence.

Mr Lawrence sat down on the window seat. "I don't feel very keen," he said.

Mrs Lawrence put back the vanity case she had just drawn from sheet after sheet of tissue paper.

"Funny," she said, "I feel sort of flat too, not a bit Christmassy."

Through the open door they could see the table in the dining room being prepared for lunch. The decorations looked fine, with the little bunches of flowers amidst the silver. Round the centre was a great heap of crackers.

"I really don't know what else we could have done," said Mrs Lawrence suddenly.

Mr Lawrence did not answer. He arose and began walking up and down the

room. Mrs Lawrence straightened the evergreen behind a picture.

"After all, they didn't ask for anything," said Mrs Lawrence. "The man would have said," went on Mrs Lawrence, "if the woman had been very ill, or the baby. I'm sure they were both all right. They are so tough, that race."

Mr Lawrence took out a cigar from his waistcoat pocket and put it back again.

"They'll be much better off in the Jewish hospital than they would have been here," said Mrs Lawrence, "— proper nursing and everything. We couldn't possibly have coped with it. Besides, going off in a hurry like that, so independent, we did not have a chance to suggest a thing."

Mr Lawrence picked up a book and then shut it. Mrs Lawrence kept twisting and untwisting the belt on her dress.

"Of course," she said hurriedly, "I shall go and enquire how they are, and take fruit and things, and perhaps some warm woollies, and ask if there is anything else they want. I'd go this morning, only I have to take the children to church..."

And then the door opened and the children came into the room.

"I've got my new necklace on," said Marigold. "Bob hasn't anything new to wear." She pirouetted round on her toes. "Hurry up, Mummy, we shall be late, and we shall miss seeing all the people come in."

 "I hope they sing 'Hark the Herald Angels' " said Bob. "We learnt the words in school and I shan't have to look at the

book. Why was Jesus born in a stable, Dad?"

"There wasn't room for them at the inn," said Mr Lawrence.

"Why, were they refugees?" said Marigold.

Nobody answered for a moment, and then Mrs Lawrence got up and tied her hair in front of her looking glass.

"Don't ask such a silly question, darling," she said.

Mr Lawrence threw open the window. Across the garden came the sound of the church bells. The sun shone on the clean, white frost, turning it to silver. Mr Lawrence had a funny, puzzled look on his face.

"I wish..." he began, "I wish... ." But he never finished what he was going to say, because the two cars carrying the Daly family and the Collins family drove in at the gate and up the drive, and the children with shouts of delight were running out onto the steps and calling, "Happy Christmas, Happy Christmas!"